THE
Night
ROAD

THE
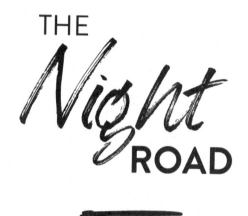
ROAD

KEVIN LUCIA

CEMETERY DANCE PUBLICATIONS

Baltimore

2022

FIRST EDITION

Trade Paperback Edition   ISBN 978-1-58767-815-8

Cemetery Dance Publications
132-B Industry Lane
Unit 7
Forest Hill, MD 21050
Email: info@cemeterydance.com

www.cemeterydance.com

1

GRACE is running through the woods and for some reason she feels uneasy, which is strange. Normally she doesn't mind running along the access roads mapping the woods around Clifton Heights, but just now, she doesn't like it. She's not sure why. It feels a little too cool. It's a bit too dark. She's not sure whether it's day or night. That makes her nervous. Scared, even.

And she's not sure where she is, exactly. The access road is lined on both sides with endless stands of Adirondack pine, so she could be anywhere. It looks vaguely familiar as it winds its way through the trees, but she just can't place it.

She's run this road before, however. She knows it. But she can't remember where it leads, or what's waiting for her at the end.

It scares her, though. With each thudding step and heartbeat, her unease escalates into full-blown fear. She's running toward something horrible. She feels this deep in her soul. But no matter how hard she tries, she can't stop putting one foot in front of the other. Can't stop pumping her arms as her relentless stride carries her effortlessly down the path toward some darkly glimmering thing which fills her with dread, but also promises a release of sorts...a terrible, wonderful release...

"MISS Donaldson?"

Grace Donaldson blinked and sat up from her slumped position too quickly, sending a jolt of pain arrowing down her neck. She grunted and closed her eyes, confused and disoriented, unsure for a moment where she was. A fuzzy image of a strange yet familiar access road winding through the woods lingered in her thoughts, but she wasn't running. She was sitting in a chair. Had fallen asleep in it, actually, and...

"Miss?"

Grace opened her eyes to see the concerned face of a young female nurse dressed in floral scrubs standing

over her. Reality hit her with a cruel backhand, and she sighed. No, she wasn't running. She was in a hospital room at Utica General. In her sister Lilly's room.

"I'm very sorry Miss Donaldson, but visiting hours will be ending in ten minutes." The nurse placed a gentle hand on her shoulder. "Are you all right?"

A stupid question, but Grace managed to swallow down a sarcastic remark. The young woman was only doing her job, after all. The staff had been more than accommodating, even putting up with Aunt Joy's aimless pestering with benevolent tolerance. She couldn't blame the nurse in any way.

She could only blame herself.

"I'm fine," Grace muttered, rubbing her face. "Thanks."

The nurse (whose badge read "Mindy") smiled. She squeezed Grace's shoulder, straightened and left. Grace cracked her neck, stood and slowly approached the bed in the middle of the room, where Lilly lay.

She stood at her sister's bedside, gripping the cool metal bedrail. She couldn't make herself look at Lilly's face. Not right now. Instead, she dug into her pocket and pulled out a silver pendant on a chain. She gazed at the charm—a disc with designs etched onto it—trying not to think about Lilly, about Aunt Joy...or about *him*. She tried not to think about *anything* but the necklace itself.

Lilly had started wearing it almost religiously two months before. Grace often caught her unconciously rubbing the pendant between her thumb and forefinger whenever she was distracted or thinking. According to Lilly, the necklace and its pendant wasn't worth much. She'd bought it on a whim from Clifton Heights' used junk shop, Handy's Pawn and Thrift. Regardless, for whatever reason, Lilly wore it everywhere. Even to bed.

Grace gripped the necklace. She'd brought it here every day over the past four weeks. It seemed ridiculous, but she somehow thought Lilly would want it near. Of course, Grace hadn't needed the nurses to tell her Lilly couldn't wear the necklace, with the wires connected to her, and the intubation tube down her throat. Grace settled for bringing it here, in a juvenile hope it might bring Lilly back. Deep inside, however, she knew that was unlikely. Still, she clung to the notion in spite of its fancy, if for nothing else than to keep her sane.

Emotion surged inside. Grace closed her eyes and clenched the chain in her fist, swallowing her despair and guilt. She should've seen this coming. She should've done something when she'd had the chance.

Now, she could do nothing but watch and wait. And run, when she couldn't watch anymore.

Grace breathed in again. She opened her eyes and without looking at Lilly, turned and left to go home, where she knew she'd only sleep fitfully, dreaming of running along a road she knew, but couldn't remember.

2

7:00 AM

GRACE fought a yawn as she laced up her running shoes and ignored her ringing smartphone. She'd slept poorly again last night, her dreams shot through with the same eerie visions of running through the woods along a strangely familiar access road she couldn't quite place. Now, she felt weirdly tense and worn out at the same time. She couldn't lie still enough to sleep anymore, yet she felt exhausted.

It didn't help matters that her smartphone had been ringing all morning. She was deeply conflicted. She could always silence it or turn it off, but then she'd grapple with the overwhelming paranoia that she might miss the inevitable call from Dr. Fitzgerald, the one she feared but expected with dread anticipation.

So far, however, none of the calls had been from Dr. Fitzgerald. The first had been from Aunt Joy, at the ungodly hour of five in the morning. Grace hadn't answered it. The other calls had been from *him*, and quite frankly? He could go to hell.

But it had kept ringing. Over and over. Every ten minutes or so it'd ring, then fall into a silence which would only prove temporary. Again, she would just switch it off, if it weren't for the fear she'd miss a call from Dr. Fitzgerald.

Blessedly, the smartphone fell silent once more as she started lacing her other shoe. As if to mock her relief, however, it started right back up. She finished lacing her shoe, put her head in her hands and simply sat there, willing her smartphone to fall silent.

It kept ringing.

Something stretched tight inside her, then snapped. Though she knew only a few more rings would send the call to voicemail, she sat up and snatched the phone off the bed. When she saw it *was* him, anger pulsed through her. It would only make things worse, but she answered the call anyway.

"Stop it," she snapped. "If you call me again, I'm going to report you. I don't care *how* much you've done for me. I'll make sure everyone knows the truth."

"*Please, Grace. I don't want to bother you. I just need...*"

"Don't call me again. Or swear to God, I'll call the police and tell them *everything.*"

"*You won't. Not after everything I've done for you, after all we've been through...*"

She hung up, seething with an anger which burned deep in her guts. Grace tossed her smartphone onto the bed and got up to leave...

She stopped, her gaze falling on Lilly's necklace, which had somehow ended up on her bed, next to where she'd tossed her phone. She frowned, confusion blunting some of her anger. How'd Lilly's necklace get there? She dimly remembered laying it on the lamp-stand next to her bed last night before turning in. How it had gotten on her bed, she'd no idea...but as she looked at it, Grace felt her anger leak away. A curious, detached peace filled her. She knew without a shadow of a doubt she should wear it. It made no sense, and she had no idea where the thought came from. But it felt right, all the same.

She scooped the necklace off the bed. Unhooked its clasp and put it on. She tucked the silver disc of the chain under her shirt. The metal felt oddly warm against her skin, not cool like she'd expected. Also, with the touch of the disc, more of her anger faded. As if the pendant were drawing it out of her, into itself.

A ridiculous thought. She shook off the strange feeling, raked her fingers through her hair and headed for the front door.

There had been a time when Grace loved running more than anything else. Loved feeling her arms and legs pumping in time with the thudding of her heart. Her footfalls sending pleasant shock-waves through her calves, up into her thighs, as everything worked together in machine-like precision.

Today; however, as she left her duplex in Hartwig Court and turned onto Hyland Avenue, she struggled to find her rhythm. Her little sister Lilly was dying. Wasting away at Utica General Hospital. There wasn't anything she could do about it, except run. Even worse...it was *her* fault Lilly was dying.

Dr. Fitzgerald—tall, athletic and far too young-looking, with his shock of unruly red hair and dancing blue eyes—had been kind, considerate and diligent in his care of Lilly. He'd treated Grace's emotions carefully, while not shielding her from the harsh truth. He'd told her the facts of the situation with the empathy of a physician twice his age and experience.

The facts were this: Lilly's brain had been deprived of oxygen for too long. There was no way of knowing for sure *how* long, but at least long enough for her to sustain significant damage to her brain stem and cerebellum. Yes, they'd stabilized her for now. Yes, she was breathing, but only with the aid of a respirator. Her pulse had been faint to the point of nonexistence upon admission. They also hadn't detected any brain activity since.

Dr. Fitzgerald said there wasn't anything left to do. They could wait, but Lilly could exist indefinitely like this, with machines breathing for her. Maybe, miraculously, she'd start breathing on her own again, and wake up. Even if she did, with the extent of the brain damage, she'd lead a vastly diminished life.

Most likely, Dr. Fitzgerald reasoned, her already weakened heart would give out from the strain. Perhaps in a few days. Maybe a few weeks. But in the end...

So Grace had waited. With her parents dead, she was Lilly's lone healthcare proxy. Only she could make the call regarding Lilly's life-support. Despite Dr. Fitzgerald's dim prospects and Aunt Joy calling her a fool...Grace had waited. At Lilly's bedside, every day, going on four weeks. Sitting and waiting. Even though she knew it was pointless, she couldn't make herself give the order to turn off Lilly's life-support.

Of course, there was that *other* thing Dr. Fitzgerald wanted to talk about. The complications of Lilly's condition, which was putting an additional strain on her system.

Despite all his gentle urging, however, Grace declined to discuss it. Had refused to acknowledge it, even.

Her instructors at Webb Community College had granted her a leave of absence, though it wouldn't have mattered to Grace if they hadn't. For now, she was done with school. Writing pointless essays regurgitating her professors' opinions held no appeal for her. Even though she'd been given an extension on all her assignments, she wasn't planning on completing them. She didn't see the point.

She'd quit the cross-country team also, yet she was running harder every day, needing a bigger and bigger adrenaline high to numb the pain and guilt. She'd realized early on in her bedside vigil that she couldn't sit there all day in the hospital, staring at nothing.

She hated looking at Lilly's pale, thin face. Her closed eyes. Her stiff, doll-like hair. So, in addition to her morning run, at noon Grace went home to run, because that's when the nurses came in to bathe Lilly and change her bed linens, and Grace couldn't stand watching them.

Following her afternoon run she returned to the hospital and stayed with Lilly until visiting hours ended. Then she again returned to their duplex, changed and ran. At night, despite running herself to exhaustion, Grace slept fitfully. Every night, she drifted through the same uneasy dream of running along a strangely familiar access road through the woods. The next day it was the same. Rinse, repeat, redo.

Every single day.

—

SHE cruised down Main Street, passing dark, empty stores and buildings not yet open for the day's business. The only sound in the early morning hush was her rhythmic footfalls on the sidewalk, which beat out a steady tattoo nearly matching her heartbeat and breath.

Ahead she saw a jogger dressed in black, running toward her on the opposite side of Shelby Road, which Main Street eventually turned into as it left town. Grace couldn't see much of the runner, just that she looked athletic and female.

Two minutes later, the runner in black seemingly vanished.

Surprise rippled through Grace, so powerfully she nearly stopped running. Her stride faltered and she misstepped, but she recovered her balance. Where'd the runner in black go? Grace didn't remember looking away, but she must've. The runner couldn't have *actually* disappeared. She must've made a sudden change of direction when Grace wasn't looking. Instead of turning left onto Old Barstow Road like she usually did, Grace picked up her pace and sped down Main Street to where it turned into Shelby Road, drawn by an odd need to see where the runner in black had gone.

Roughly a hundred feet outside town she saw the answer. Shelby Road Cemetery, on her left. An access road ran from its entrance to the tree line. The runner must've turned down it and cut through the cemetery, heading toward the woods…

There.

Grace saw a black form melt into the woods, as if the trees and brush had swallowed her up.

follow her

She pulled up parallel to Shelby Road Cemetery's gates, running in place.

follow her

why?

She didn't know.

Grace stared down the access road, which disappeared into the woods. Darkness loomed in the almost mouth-like space where the road passed into the tree line. Grace shivered, and though it was probably her imagination, it felt like Lilly's necklace—the pendant, in particular—tingled against her skin.

For the life of her, she couldn't remember a funeral procession ever coming there. She didn't know why it wasn't used anymore. It just wasn't. There was no one in charge of maintaining the grounds, which lay in disrepair, overgrown with weeds. Many of the headstones were cracked and broken, and the road...

Grace looked down the road again (which seemed oddly worn with use, now that she thought about it, in comparison with the rest of the grounds and the nearly collapsed caretaker's shed). The runner in black had gone down this road, disappearing into the woods. She herself had never run this road before, and abruptly found herself wondering where it led. For some strange reason she couldn't put her finger on, she wanted to find out.

She ran in place, feet thudding the ground, heart beating, breathing frosty plumes into the chilly morning air, staring down the road.

What the hell?

Why not?

What else did she have to do today? Sit in Lilly's hospital room and stare at nothing all morning? Ten or fifteen minutes tacked onto her running time wasn't going to make any difference in her day. And if Lilly passed away while she was running...?

So be it.

Grace crossed Shelby Road and entered the cemetery.

THE instant Grace crossed the threshold from the cemetery into the woods, the temperature dropped several degrees, the thick stands of Adirondack pine blocking out most of the morning sun. Even so, she could see the road ahead clearly. She again wondered at how well-used it looked. Of course, county vehicles were always using access roads like this to get into the woods for one reason or another. She'd run on many of those over the years. She supposed this one was no different.

There.

Up ahead.

The mysterious runner in black, ascending a hill in the road. It was defintely a female, Grace thought, wearing her black hair in a ponytail, which flashed as she ran. The runner crested the hill and disappeared over it.

A strange urgency filled Grace, flushing her with adrenaline. She sped up, heart beating faster. She didn't know why she wanted to catch up with the runner so bad; didn't understand her compulsive need to learn who the runner was, but she gave into it, freely. She sped down the road, trees flashing by in green blurs. When she hit the hill's incline she didn't slow. She lengthened her stride, pumping her arms harder.

Somewhere inside, a small part of her understood why she was following the runner, why she was giving in to her need. For this brief moment, she wasn't thinking

about Lilly, Aunt Joy, or *him*. She was running, she *was* the running, and that was all. That was enough.

Grace crested the hill and saw the runner in black, who seemed much farther ahead than should be possible. She disappeared around a bend, black ponytail flashing.

Grace sped up, but the road sloped downward, steeper than she'd expected it to. Her steps faltered and her ankle twisted slightly, but she reigned herself in, narrowly avoiding a stumble. She slowed, bringing herself under control at the bottom. As the road leveled out, her stride lengthened again. She increased her pace, determined to catch the mysterious runner in black. She wanted to talk to her, ask her *where* she was going, where the path lead…

A *screech* jarred her rhythm.

Grace slid to a stop, staring at the sight before her. "Holy…*shit*."

Sitting on a stump alongside the path, about ten feet away was the biggest crow she'd ever seen. More the size of an eagle than anything else. She didn't know anything about birds, much less crows, but she didn't think crows *could* get this big. It looked impossibly broad across the breast. Its beak seemed much longer than normal.

It *screeched* again, spreading its wings in an impressive span. Again, she thought, more like an eagle or a larger bird of prey. She felt a little surprised at the small spike of fear jabbing her stomach, surprised even more to suddenly find herself digging Lilly's necklace out from under her shirt, clutching the pendant, as if it were a cross and the crow a vampire.

The crow rustled its feathers, glaring at her with piercing golden eyes.

Glaring.

Warning?

It was stupid to attribute such a human trait to an animal, but that's how Grace felt. It was *warning* her against going any further. She squeezed the pendant tighter.

A sudden rebelliousness rose inside. It was a bird. A freaking crow. That's all. It wasn't an omen, a monster, or dangerous at all. Just a really large bird. Yes, a bird with incredibly sharp-looking talons and a hooked beak which could probably do some serious damage…

But it was just a bird.

She stepped forward; still aware she was holding the pendant, somehow unable to let it go.

The crow screeched louder and leaped down, wings spread, its span covering most of the road. Grace thought again how *angry* it looked, glaring at her with those eyes. It almost seemed as if it were *daring* her to go further. She wasn't about to be scared off by a bird, though. That was ridiculous, it was…

God.

Who the hell *cared?*

With that, Grace abruptly came back to her senses. Without her phone, she had no idea what time it was. Despite her earlier decision, that if Lilly passed while she was running, it was meant to be...what if Dr. Fitzgerald *had* called with the news that Lilly finally...

no

don't think about it

"Screw this," she muttered. Hands clenched at her sides, Grace turned away from the crow. It didn't make another sound as she walked away, back toward Shelby Road Cemetery. Within a few steps she was running again, though stiffer, now, her rhythm lost.

3

8:00 AM

AFTER showering and dressing, Lilly's necklace hanging reassuringly from her neck, Grace stood before her "Wall of Fame." All of Grace's track and cross-country plaques hung on the wall around a shelf filled with trophies. When they'd first moved in together, Grace had tried to throw them out. They'd never meant much to her. Running was what mattered. Not material things like trophies, medals, ribbons, plaques, or newspaper clippings. She ran for the experience of running; the breathing and the pounding of her heart. The trembling of her thighs and calves, and the interior place she traveled to when she was in her groove. That's what mattered. Far as she was concerned, her awards belonged in the trash.

Lilly wouldn't have it. She'd insisted Grace keep them. She'd even taken the initiative to arrange them on the wall in something which unnervingly reminded Grace of a *shrine*, of all things. Lilly had run cross-country and track also but she hadn't enjoyed the same success, nor had she ever loved running like Grace did. But she'd been Grace's biggest fan. When Grace complained about all the attention she got, Lilly was the first to say she deserved it. She said Grace was just like Dad, the best runner in Webb County Cross Country history.

When Grace wanted to quit her junior year, Lilly hadn't let her.

When Grace didn't believe in herself, Lilly quietly bolstered her. She was always the loudest to cheer, was always there to encourage her on the rare occasions when she didn't win. When Grace didn't feel like training, Lilly mildly admonished her, pushing Grace to do her best. In all these things, Lilly had been a stand-in for Mom, Dad and especially Aunt Joy.

Lilly was the reason for these awards. *She* had pushed Grace to be the best she could be, to *win*.

But what had Grace done in return?

Betrayed her.

THE *Night* ROAD

In payment for all her support and encouragement, Grace had turned her back on Lilly when her little sister had needed her most. Lilly never said anything about Grace's betrayal. Never hinted she'd known about it, or used that hint as a weapon to get things from Grace. But it was there, it had happened, and as the years passed, it had germinated quietly, until it finally came to dreadful bloom four weeks ago.

Grace shuddered and tore herself away from the hated trophies and plaques. They were coming down. She'd throw the plaques and trophies into a barrel, burn them, and love every minute of watching the wood turn to ash and the metal blacken. She'd save the newspaper clippings—collected by Lilly, arranged with care in several scrapbooks—for last. She'd throw them on top, and watch the clippings disintegrate.

Grace collected her things, grabbed her car keys off the kitchen table and headed for the door. She tried to ignore the ugliness simmering inside her. An ugliness she had spawned. As her hand closed on the doorknob, she felt a sudden, aching need to run again. To purge herself of the ugliness inside...but also, to run out to Shelby Road Cemetery and see where the access road went, to see if the runner in black was still there.

It was a near thing. She teetered on the edge of heeding her strange impulse to investigate the access road.

Twisting the doorknob, for a moment she didn't know which she'd pick: the hospital and waiting at Lilly's bedside, or running, and the access road.

As she opened the door, she felt her guilt swell. She'd already run this morning. She needed to be at Lilly's side. To try in vain to cancel a debt she didn't believe she could ever repay. The mystery of the runner in black and the access road would have to wait until later.

10:00 AM

AT the hospital, sitting next to Lilly, Grace tried vainly to read a survival thriller called *Ascent*, by Ronald Malfi. Mostly, she wanted to occupy her mind. It wasn't working. She forgot character dialogue and exposition as soon as she read them, getting confused over setting description and plot points. Sentences seemed strung together from bits of nonsense she couldn't decipher. Eventually, she gave up with a sigh, closed the book, bent over and stuffed it into the satchel sitting at her feet.

It was getting close to noon. Nearly time for another run. Soon as the thought entered her head, the access road through Shelby Road Cemetery flashed through her mind, along with the runner in black. Something stirred inside her that she hadn't felt in what seemed like forever: anticipation. Eagerness. The thought of discovering what lay at the end of that access road intrigued her. Maybe even *excited* her, for God's sake. She instantly felt guilty feeling such things at Lilly's beside.

She gathered her things and stood. Approached Lilly's bed, holding herself very still inside. Always slight to begin with, Lilly had lost so much weight the past few weeks. She now looked like a skeleton, with her frozen, hollowed-out cheeks and her stiff blond hair, no longer shiny and full. Lilly looked so thin and insubstantial, Grace couldn't help imagining that if she touched her, Lilly would crumble to dust.

Her fault.

It was her fault.

If only she'd paid more attention. If only she'd been looking for the signs. No matter how she tried to deny it, Lilly dying in this bed was Grace's fault.

Grace's stomach clenched. Spontaneously, she reached for Lilly's hand…

Someone cleared their throat and coughed, making a rasping, masculine sound.

Grace thought it was Dr. Fitzgerald. She prepared herself for whatever news he might have. Perhaps Lilly's organs were failing as her heart weakened even more. Or, maybe he wanted to talk about that other thing again…

The worst part?

Grace didn't know which she feared the most.

As she turned, however, she didn't see Dr. Fitzgerald, she saw…

Him.

Standing in the doorway, his eyes flickering like a scared animal's. His posture was stiff and tense, as if he were poised on the brink of flight.

For a moment Grace stared, convinced she was hallucinating. He couldn't be that stupid. To show up here, despite her threat?

Apparently he was. Worse, he took her momentary speechlessness as an invitation to speak. He held up his hands and whispered, "I shouldn't be here. I know that. But we *have* to talk." He stepped forward. "Please. I need to know one thing, and then I promise…"

How dare he?

She forced her face into an expressionless mask. Swallowed her anger and, yes, the nearly overwhelming guilt and self-disgust she felt at just the *sight* of him. "Get *out*. Now."

His pained expression looked genuine, as if he really cared and was hurt by her anger. She knew the truth, however. She knew what he was *really* like. What kind of monster he hid inside. She'd seen it. In the flesh.

"Listen, I…"

She dug into her pocket, pulled out her phone and held it up. "Get out. Or I call the police."

His pleading expression faded. It was replaced by a carefully neutral one which hinted more truthfully at the predatory nature he masked from the world with his trademark, easy-going grin. "They won't believe you."

She gritted her teeth and forced herself to speak quietly. "It doesn't matter. Once I start talking people will listen to what I tell them, and then it will spread. You know how this town works. Everyone will be talking about it by the end of tomorrow. Whether they believe it or not."

He backed up, surrendering. He dropped his hands and said in an emotionless voice, "It doesn't have to be this way. All I need is for you to tell me the truth, and then I'll never speak to you ever again. It *doesn't* have to be this way."

She shook her head, amazed not only at the depths of his arrogance but also that she'd never seen it, for so many years. "It was *always* going to be this way."

He stared for a heartbeat longer.

She gestured again with her phone.

He shook his head. "You're making a mistake." He turned, left the doorway, and walked away.

Grace waited.

After several tense minutes, she slowly dropped her guard as the doorway remained empty and he didn't return. She turned and grasped the pendant hanging from Lilly's necklace, gripping it tightly. Sobbing quietly, shoulders shaking, her tears fell on Lilly's pale and thin hand, so still on the white sheet covering her. For a moment, Grace nurtured the fantasy that—like in a Disney or Hallmark movie—her tears hitting Lilly's hand would magically awaken her. But when she released the pendant and took Lilly's hand, it felt limp, and damp with her tears, and nothing more.

———

GRACE drove home slowly, her mind quiet and numb. She felt far away from herself and the reality of her driving along Route 28 North. She passed Whitelake and then Old Forge, paying little attention to her surroundings, slowing down along Old Forge's main thoroughfare through force of habit alone.

She realized, in a hazy sort of way, that she was retreating more and more deeply inside herself as the days passed. Disconnecting with her surroundings and her life. If she wasn't sitting at Lilly's bedside or running, nothing seemed real. In an abstract way, a part of her mind noted this as a concern. She pushed it aside, however, as too emotionally draining to think about, and continued to drive.

As she was turning off Route 28 North to Clifton Heights, a small sliver of fear jabbed her heart. She thought she saw a restored red 1974 Chevy pickup following her. It continued past the turn-off, however.

he's not that stupid, he couldn't be

could he?

Grace shook her head and picked up her speed, nonetheless. What she needed right now was to run. Once she was running, everything would be fine.

———

1:00 PM

STANDING before the "Wall of Fame," Grace stared at a framed cross-country picture from her senior year. She stared at *him*, hating him with every fiber of her being. Wishing she had the strength to do something more than just threaten a call to the police. Her anger consumed her, yet she somehow felt powerless, also.

Her phone rang.

Still staring and hating, she reached into her pocket. Answered without looking, somehow knowing it wasn't *him* or her aunt.

It was Dr. Fitzgerald.

He spoke quietly and slowly, his voice sounding sympathetic and consoling, though that didn't help, at all. In matter-of-fact words, he carefully explained how the expected had finally happened, shortly after Grace left the hospital. Lilly's heart, weakened and pushed past its breaking point, had given out. They hadn't been able to revive her. As for the other thing he'd wanted to talk about, he hated to ask her again, but was there any way she could confirm…

Grace mumbled "Thank you" and hung up.

She slipped her phone back into her pocket.

Screamed and punched the framed cross-country picture, shattering the glass, knocking it off the wall.

Pain flashed across her knuckles. She held her fist up and saw several jagged slashes well up with blood. She stood still for several minutes, like a marble statue, *feeling* cold as stone, squeezing her fist, bleeding onto the floor as her hate and rage throbbed inside like a molten core. The pain from the cuts felt *good*, feeding her rage.

She grabbed the pendant hanging from Lilly's necklace and squeezed, as she'd been doing a lot since she started wearing it. The silver disc felt slick against her bloodied palm, and though she was sure it was just her imagination, warm and tingling, also.

She took a deep breath.

THE *Night* ROAD

Turned away from the Wall of Fame *Lilly* had made for her and went to the bathroom to clean and bandage her hand. She neglected to clean the blood off Lilly's pendant, however, for some reason leaving it blood-smeared and sticky.

4

BY the time Grace reached Shelby Road a part of her hated running. Her love of running had to lead to this, after all. It had led to Lilly's death.

But she wouldn't ever be able to stop. It was the only thing left in her life she could control, the only release she had. Running was the only way to rid herself of the sorrow and guilt festering inside her, the only way for her to flush it from her system. As much as she hated running at the moment, she *had* to run the pain out; run until she could no longer think or feel. Run until there wasn't anything left, until she'd sweat out all the black despair oozing inside her.

And if it stopped working? If running no longer got rid of the pain?

Something else would have to be done.

Ahead loomed Shelby Road Cemetery's gates. She ran harder. Cut left, down the access road bisecting the grounds, stumbling over ruts but not falling, lurching toward the tree line and its shadows.

Crumbled and leaning gravestones flashed by. She passed the old caretaker's shed and plunged into the woods. She stumble-lurched ahead, heart pounding, a force inside drawing her chaotic flailing into something resembling rhythmic harmony. With each step she drew herself together, gaining more control. When she reached the hill she only pushed harder. Her thighs quivered and her ankles throbbed. Her breath hitched as her lungs screamed for air, but she didn't slow down. She ignored her body, trying to run away from her pain.

As the road descended, Grace ran through the spot where she'd seen the crow yesterday. She felt none of her unease, however. Only a sudden burst of singing exhilaration. For some reason she couldn't explain, her hate of running had disappeared, along with her pain. She'd been *made* to run, after all. And she was going find out where this road led.

The trees streamed by. The only sounds were her footfalls and rhythmic breaths. A small part of her wondered why she wasn't grieving over Lilly, or why she wasn't angry at Aunt Joy or *him*, but the running drowned all other feeling. There was running, and nothing else.

Another gentle incline. She sped up it, her feet deftly adapting as she crested the small hill. It leveled off, and she saw...

Grace slowed.

Her run fading into a jog, then a walk.

The access road split into two separate lanes which ran parallel to each other. On these two lanes, it looked as if someone had picked up a small block of buildings from town and plunked them down out in the woods. She saw what looked like cabins, houses, and other buildings.

In the absence of her footfalls, the quiet swelled. As she walked, an overwhelming peace filled her. If she decided to sit in the middle of the road and soak up all the quiet, she felt as if she could easily sit for hours.

Mindful of her muscles and joints stiffening again, however, she kept walking, taking in the surreal scene before her. Plain but sturdy-looking cabins of varying sizes and styles lined both roads. Cramped front yards were overgrown with brush and cluttered with deadfall. The cabins were weathered gray, their siding mottled with black-green moss.

However, most of them were intact. A few roofs were caved in, a few porches collapsed. Of course, she had no idea what the insides of the cabins looked like. From the outside, they looked mostly intact, which created the eerie illusion that the—town? village?—had been abandoned wholesale only hours before, everyone having gotten up and walked out, en masse. Because of that, it also felt like they were due back at any moment, and would catch her trespassing.

Even more surreal, sitting on the intact porches she saw rocking chairs, looking as if someone had just vacated them and would also return shortly. Leaning against several houses were rusted old bicycles. Hanging on the sides of others were old-fashioned wooden snow sleds with metal runners. If she searched the small, overgrown lawns, would she find cast-off toys? Old baseballs and bats? Rusted toy trucks and pails? Small shovels and skeletal remains of tricycles?

Around the middle of the abandoned town, Grace encountered a long, wide building on her right which opened to both access roads. She saw what appeared to be jumbled piles of old barrels, also rows of rusted milk cans sitting on the porch, which ran the length of the building.

A general store? Grace marveled at the thought of a small, self-sustaining village in the woods outside Clifton Heights. How long had it been here? *Why* was it here? When had it been abandoned? Why hadn't she ever heard anything about it?

THE *Night* ROAD

Past the "store" was another large building. Through the door, Grace saw rows of what looked like cots. The town infirmary?

Images formed in Grace's mind of what life had been like here. She imagined a close-knit community filled with children's laughter as they ran down the two roads, weaving around cabins and playing in the woods, especially during summer. She pictured young and old men sitting on porches or leaning against railings, smoking pipes and drinking beer, or maybe even moonshine from mason jars. She saw women cooking, mending clothes, tending to small flower or vegetable gardens.

She wondered what life was like during the often-unforgiving Adirondack winters. Were families able to heat their cabins with wood or coal stoves? How did they keep the access roads clear of snow? Did anyone own cars or trucks? The buildings didn't look old enough to have been built when people only used horse-drawn carts for transportation, but still. Would a visitor in the winter find deer gutted and hanging from trees behind the cabins, ready to be salted and packaged for the long, cold months ahead?

In the midst of her imagining, it occurred to her again that she wasn't thinking about Lilly being dead, Aunt Joy, or *him*. Guilt tried to rear its head, to accuse her of being selfish and uncaring. It faltered and faded in the overwhelming peace of her surroundings, which

was just fine with her. She'd have to deal with reality soon enough. She'd gone running to *not* think, and that's just what she was going to do…

A low, rasping croak came from above.

Grace spun and looked to the trees, adrenaline speeding her heart back up. She recognized that sound, of course. It really shouldn't frighten her so much because…

It was just a crow.

Perched high on a branch about fifteen feet up. Just an ordinary crow. Not the unusually large specimen she'd seen yesterday, though it looked just as menacing, ready to spring at her, claws extended and beak snapping…

And the raven, never flitting, still is sitting

The scrap of Edgar Allan Poe's famous poem (which she'd memorized in high school English) whispered unbidden in her mind. As she stared at the crow—clutching Lilly's pendant, still sticky with her blood—she couldn't help but hear *And his eyes have all the seeming of a demon's that is dreaming…*

No.

No demon. Just a stupid crow, and it's not even as big as that weird one I saw yesterday. It's just a crow, just…

With a crackling squawk and a rustle of feathers and wing, another crow lit on the branch next to the one staring at her. Despite herself, Grace yelped, squeezing Lilly's pendant even tighter.

Another squawk and fluttering, to her left. She looked and saw another crow settling onto a branch. Almost instantly, two more crows joined it, rasping and cawing.

More squawking, to her right. More crows landing and perching above her.

A medley of croaks and rasps filled the air, set to the fluttering of untold wings flapping. Soon the trees were full of them, dozens of crows perched on branches, cawing and staring at her with bright yellow eyes.

A *murder.*

A *murder of crows.*

Panic filled Grace, warring with what little common sense remained. Crows. So many of them. Had to be two or three dozen. What were they doing here? What brought them? Why were they staring at her?

"Not staring," she muttered. "Just crows. *Not* staring."

But they were.

Staring, cawing, ruffling their feathers. Dozens of night-black crows, ranging the tree branches above her. Oddly enough, they were above the village's entrance… almost as if they were sentries standing watch.

She heard cawing in the distance, and more flapping wings.

"Nope," she whispered. "No way."

Grace turned and, feeling no shame whatsoever, ran back the way she came, pushed by a strange dread (not *exactly* fear) that she'd nearly crossed some invisible boundary from which there was no return, a boundary she wasn't ready to cross.

A ridiculous notion, of course. So a bunch of crows were roosting on branches in the trees above an abandoned village in the middle of the forest. So what? It didn't *mean* anything. Just like the crow she'd seen yesterday hadn't meant anything. They were crows.

That's all.

Even so, Grace couldn't deny her unease faded as she left behind the abandoned village and the crows. The more distance she put between her and them, the calmer she felt, and yet...

And yet.

She felt incomplete somehow, as she ran back toward Shelby Road Cemetery. Her dread was fading, but so was the strange sense of *belonging* she'd felt in the abandoned village. Maybe she did feel calmer, but she also felt oddly hollow. Unrooted. Disconnected. Also, though it most likely meant nothing, she noticed Lilly's pendant felt completely normal, now. Just a cold metal disk sticky with her blood, and nothing more.

5

GRACE had found Lilly four weeks ago after cross-country practice at Webb Community College. She was shutting off her '87 Ford Escort in their duplex's driveway when her smartphone rang. It was Cassie Tillman from The Skylark Diner where both of them worked; her part time, Lilly full time. Lilly hadn't shown up for her shift, which wasn't right at all, because Lilly was always early to work. Always.

"Lilly's late," Cassie said. *"I'm worried."*

The driveway was empty, which hadn't meant anything. Lilly took a cab every Wednesday because Grace didn't get home in time from practice to take Lilly to work. Grace had offered to skip practice so she could take Lilly, but Lilly wouldn't hear of it. "You *need* to run, Grace. Without it, you wouldn't be whole. You'd be…"

like me

…was how Grace always imagined Lilly saying it. But Lilly never did. She just continued lightly, "You'd be impossible to live with if you weren't running."

Grace would always answer her, "Yeah, but you need to run too, Lil. You haven't since high school."

Of course, she never asked *why* Lilly didn't run, because she knew the answer to that question, just as Lilly did.

In response, Lilly would only smile sadly and say, "Running just isn't my thing, anymore."

Grace was on the phone with Cassie when she found Lilly. She'd already been on high alert coming through the front door, because Cassie was right. Lilly was *never* late to work, even when taking a cab. Her panic only worsened when, turning around in the den wildly, a sparkle had caught her eye. Hanging from the biggest running trophy she'd ever won—Cross-Country State Champion, her junior year—was Lilly's beloved necklace. It had been hung there. For her.

Grace knew, right then. If Lilly had left her necklace there, it had finally happened. The unspeakable thing she'd feared the last three years. There hadn't

been any signs, of course. Lilly had been acting fine (except for those occasional sad smiles), but it had finally happened. Grace knew it. Her worst nightmare had finally come true...

Grace found Lilly in her bedroom. Hanging from the ceiling fan, above an overturned chair. Somehow Grace managed to get her down. She'd performed mouth-to-mouth, called 911, performed more mouth-to-mouth, until EMS arrived. But she'd known even then that Lilly—the Lilly who mattered—was gone forever.

6

DRAINED by her manic run, her discovery of the abandoned village and her strange encounter with the crows, Grace took longer than usual to return home. It was always hard to recapture a running rhythm after stopping for only a few minutes, and she'd stopped for at least fifteen, maybe even twenty. She'd struggled on her way back through the cemetery, out onto Shelby Road and toward town. Finally, after what seemed like hours, Grace turned off Hyland and jogged stiffly into Hartwig Court. Her joints aching, she slowed to a walk, limped to her duplex and let herself in.

Lilly had never let on she thought Grace might suspect her plans, just like she never once raised the subject of

Grace's betrayal, or that she was even aware of it. However, Grace had sensed it lurking there, beneath the surface. She'd always known, somehow, that Lilly *knew* how Grace had betrayed her. And Grace had known or feared Lilly would do this, ever since her junior year, when...

No.

She clumsily closed a mental door on the memory. Overwhelmed with fatigue, she stumbled through the den to her bedroom. She didn't bother showering, changing clothes, taking off Lilly's necklace, or checking the bandage on her hand. She slipped into bed, pulled the covers over her, closed her eyes and fell into darkness.

GRACE runs, her arms pumping and her legs flying as she speeds through the woods, running along the mysterious access road which she recognizes, now. Trees and brush flash by in green smears. She can't tell if it's day or night, because the flickering glow among the looming shadows doesn't look like daylight or moonlight, but something else. Something powerful. Something bigger.

Her feet pound in time to the rhythms of her heartbeat, echoing her breaths, which shudder through her effortlessly. All is good, all is right, all is bliss, so long as she runs along this night road, for that's what this is.

THE *Night* ROAD

The night road. She doesn't know what that means, she just knows it feels right, deep inside. As she runs, Lilly's pendant burns against her skin, neither cold nor hot, sending waves of strength through her.

Someone dressed in black is running ahead of her. Her long black hair flashes in a ponytail. Hope surges through Grace, tinged with a desperate sense of grief. She needs to catch the runner in black. Why, she doesn't know. But she must catch the runner in black. She must.

Grace speeds up effortlessly and feels as if she's flying now, her feet gliding over the night road. The distance between her and the runner shortens ever so slightly. For a tantalizing moment, it seems like she'll catch up. She can see the runner's bright yellow sneakers flashing in golden blurs. She runs harder.

The runner in black pulls away, speeding up and disappearing over the rise leading to the strange abandoned town. Despair explodes inside Grace. She knows she can't catch up, no matter how hard she runs. Even so, she can't quit. She runs impossibly fast now, arms and legs pumping, feet gliding. In a blink of an eye she's clearing the rise into the abandoned town...

And she comes to an abrupt stop, skidding in the dirt, no longer flying but rooted in awe.

People.

Everywhere.

Filling the streets of the abandoned town, which is no longer abandoned, but bustling with all kinds of people, of all ages, wearing clothes which look several decades out of fashion. The men in dungarees, overalls and boots, wearing straw hats, many with unshaven cheeks bristling with stubble. The woman in simple gingham dresses without frills.

Everyone looks happy and carefree. Young men and old lounge on cabin porches, lean against railings, or sit in wooden chairs, smoking pipes and cigarettes, drinking from brown glass bottles in paper bags. They look like they're relaxing after a hard day's work.

Children run down the street, or ride old bicycles. A group of children chase a rolling wooden hoop, batting it with sticks as they run alongside. Down the other street, Grace sees another group of children playing with a tire, rolling a child inside as they laugh and cheer.

Slowly, Grace walks down the street to her left. She passes men sitting on porches and women tending small gardens in likewise small front yards. Many look up and offer friendly smiles, nodding and waving as she passes. There is no suspicion or surprise in their expressions, only warm welcome. As if they recognize her. As if she belongs, and is long waited for.

As she walks, Grace looks closely at the women. They're all working. Some tending gardens, washing clothes in iron tubs and hanging them on lines strung between trees. Others are sweeping porches, maneuvering around the men who talk, smoke and drink.

Not all the men are sitting and talking. Some climb ladders to work on roof shingles or to fix windows. Others work under the hoods of old trucks which look twenty or even thirty years old. Not every cabin has a vehicle parked before it—more like every two or three—and as she passes a cabin, a truck rattles to life. It pulls slowly out onto the access road and drives away, its cab and bed filled with men. This must be how they travel. In groups, sharing rides.

Grace looks down the street, searching for the runner in black. The despair she feels at losing the runner still lingers, but it's dampened by the joy pulsing through the crowd. Children laugh and shout, men and women talk, some of the men whistle as they work, the women hum to themselves. As Grace passes a small clearing on her left between two cabins, men sit around a barrel-fire, slapping their knees and singing uproariously as another man plays something that looks like bagpipes.

As she walks, folks continue to smile and nod at her. Smoke curls from chimneys. Lanterns suffuse the street with a soft, yellow-orange glow. Grace realizes it's dusk, almost nighttime. Outside cabins she sees more barrel-fires, their flickers sending dancing shadows onto the ground. Grace feels it could turn pitch-black and this town would still burn brightly against the night, so long as their fires burn.

Unconsciously, she reaches up and grasps Lilly's pendant, which throbs warmly against her skin. Grace wonders idly where the runner in black has gone, but she feels much less concerned about it than she did before.

She passes children playing. Some are skipping rope, chanting a rhyme she can't quite hear. Others squat on the ground, shooting marbles, while still others play jacks.

She hears something.

A cry.

Something like a wail, waxing and waning above the happy sounds of community. There one moment, gone the next. Icy dread trickles down her neck. Grace listens closely, but the sound isn't repeated...

Shock ripples through Grace, almost halting her fast. On her right is a long building, its porch full of barrels and burlap bags filled with maybe flour, or seed. The runner in black ducks past those barrels and into the store, ponytail flashing as it vanishes through a doorway.

A pulsing need rises in Grace. She walks quickly, leaving the road, mounting the porch and pushing through the same door. A jingling bell announces her arrival.

She's in the general store. It looks like textbook pictures she remembers from history class in high school. In

the middle of the store sits a large black cast iron stove. Orange glows behind its grate. A gentle warmth soaks into her skin.

Next to the stove several men sit in rickety wooden chairs, two of them playing chess. The pieces are hand-carved and simple. The other men smoke and drink clear liquid from glass jars, talking in low, meditative tones. One or two look up as Grace passes by, offering amiable nods. She nods back, but absently, seeking the runner in black.

Past the iron stove are several rows of shelves neatly ordered by category. Canned and boxed goods. Tools and hardware. Neatly folded clothes, boots and shoes. Grace moves quickly down a row of basic hardware supplies—featuring jars of nails, screws, nuts and bolts— sure the runner in black has just slipped out of the row. She hurries toward the sales counter, which is busy with customers and their purchases.

Against the counter are barrels filled with an endless assortment of candies, individually wrapped in brightly colored papers: reds, oranges, yellows, browns, pinks, and blues. Above the barrels on the counter are racks of the biggest peppermint sticks she's ever seen.

Grace scans the crowd at the counter, looking for the runner in black, sure she came this way. Behind the counter is a wall of cubby-holes filled with rolls of different kinds of fabric. A young woman turns from the wall with a roll of denim. She smiles at Grace, lips forming words Grace can't hear. Grace shakes her head, trying to ask about the runner in black, has anyone seen someone dressed in all black, and where did she go? but nothing comes out. The young woman smiles and nods, then turns her attention back to her customer, unrolling the fabric and measuring it.

Grace hears the wailing again.

Louder than before, but still faint, like she's hearing it through layers of gauze. The cry grips her heart with icy fear. No one in the store seems to notice as they go about their business. Grace moves past them toward the exit, and sees the runner in black go out the door.

Grace pushes past milling customers who pay no heed to her passage. She leaves the store, following the runner in black out onto the road, toward the wail, which hasn't faded this time. In fact, it's growing stronger as she follows it.

Her walk turns into a brisk jog. She catches glimpses of the runner moving past people in the road. The wail is much louder, now. Her heart speeds up, an unreasoning fear washing away her peace. She knows that wail, somehow. She knows who makes it.

The runner ducks past a small group of men, once again speeding up impossibly fast. Grace breaks into a run after her. The crowds are much thinner here, but still the runner always seems to dart behind small knots of people talking and walking. They're oblivious to the runner, and Grace, too, as she weaves among them.

The wailing is no longer distant or muffled. It is a piercing woman's cry of pain and misery. Grace's fear swells into panicked hysteria as she nears a long building similar to the store. That's where the wailing is coming from. People crowd one of the doors.

The runner in black slips by them and enters the building.

Grace mounts the porch and rushes for the door. The people clustered there still don't acknowledge her, but they move aside and part, as if they sense her presence, unconsciously.

Grace crosses the threshold into the building. It's the infirmary. Cots line the walls. Most of them are empty, save the nearest. Around which are three women and a man who looks like a country doctor from an old black-and-white movie. A black bag sitting on the floor and the old-fashioned stethoscope hanging from his neck completes the picture.

The women comfort a patient, a much younger woman lying on the cot. One stands behind, holding up her head and shoulders with one hand, pressing a folded wet cloth onto her forehead with the other. The other two women sit on either side of the patient, each holding a hand. Though Grace can't hear their words, the motions they make are comforting.

Midwives, Grace thinks. Very abruptly she understands what she's seeing. The woman supporting the patient's head. The other two holding her hands and speaking softly. The doctor sitting on a stool at the end of the cot. The patient's legs elevated and spread, with a bucket on the floor underneath the patient's pelvis area. Though she can't see into the bucket (and doesn't want to) its rim and the floor around it is splattered with red and clear fluids. The patient's belly is full.

Grace senses movement at the corner of her vision. It's the runner in black, standing off to the side, watching the scene as Grace is. Grace wants to go to her, talk to her, *confront* her, find out who she is. She can't, however. She's mesmerized by the scene before her, and can't tear away her gaze.

The patient's belly quivers and her legs shake. She *screams*, her head thrashing side to side. The women holding her hands continue their assurances but the pregnant patient takes no comfort in their words. The midwives place their hands on either shoulder, trying to hold her still. Grace can hear the doctor speaking calmly (not the actual words, just the sounds), trying to reassure the patient also, but obviously in vain.

She screams.

There's a liquid *tearing* sound.

Grace cries out as blood and other fluids spurt over the doctor's hands and into the bucket and onto the floor. No one notices Grace's cry, except the pregnant woman, who rolls her head in Grace's direction and gazes at her...

The runner in black moves. Walks slowly to the pregnant woman, who at first doesn't acknowledge the runner's presence. An iron fist squeezes Grace's heart and lungs. She opens her mouth, but she can't speak.

The patient stares at Grace.

The runner in black stops at the patient's bedside and lays a hand (which is also black, as if she's wearing a full bodysuit of some kind) on the patient's shoulder. She extends her other hand, clearly wishing the patient to release the midwife's hand and take hers.

The patient looks at Grace, her gaze pleading, imploring.

Grace tries to speak, to tell her no, don't take her hand! but even as her throat works, the words are locked there, useless.

The patient slowly looks away from Grace and to the runner in black. Lets go of the midwife's hand and takes the runner's. Almost instantly she breaks into convulsions. There's another liquid tearing sound and the patient throws her head back and screams while the doctor barks sharp commands and the midwives try to hold her down. Grace finally finds her voice and screams too as a shrill ringing fills her ears…

7

A shrill ringing fills her ears...

Grace blinked slowly, her eyelids heavy with sleep. Her mind struggled, sluggish, as if she were heavily drugged. She rolled over and peered at the digital clock on her nightstand. Bright green numbers read 5:00 against a black background.

Grace closed her eyes and pressed her face into the bed-sheets, her mind still foggy. She vaguely remembered going to sleep around three in the afternoon the previous day. Had she actually slept fifteen hours? Had she dreamed? Of running somewhere, chasing the runner in black down the access road, to the abandoned village, new and alive with people, and...

No.

More ringing. Her smartphone, next to the clock. Somehow sensing whomever was calling would only keep trying, Grace snaked her hand to the nightstand and grabbed her smartphone. She answered with a mumbled, "'llo?"

"Finally. I've been calling since last night. What's wrong with you?"

Aunt Joy.

Oh, God.

It was Aunt Joy. She'd found out about Lilly. Grace hadn't called Aunt Joy to tell her, and Aunt Joy had found out on her own.

Grace didn't answer, the wheels in her head still turning slowly. She licked her lips and opened her mouth to speak, but before she could, Aunt Joy continued.

"Dead. Dead yesterday afternoon. Your own sister, and you didn't call anyone to let them know. Didn't call me. Your aunt."

The fog which had been clouding her thoughts evaporated. She felt spent and oddly sore, as if she'd just finished running. She was awake now, however. And to be honest, Aunt Joy was right. She *hadn't* called anyone. She'd lost it and run away into the woods. Afterward she'd come home, tumbled into bed and promptly fallen asleep without letting anyone know Lilly had died.

THE *Night* ROAD

Dr. Fitzgerald had probably called Aunt Joy some-time last night. Procedure or something, she figured. Aunt Joy *was* Lilly's nearest next of kin after her. Didn't they need to get the body to the funeral home right away? Grace thought she'd heard that somewhere, or had numbly discussed it with Dr. Fitzgerald, and then forgotten.

Anyway, Dr. Fitzgerald had most likely mentioned to Aunt Joy that he'd called Grace first. Aunt Joy would've realized Grace had known and *hadn't* called her. No wonder she was pissed. Oh, God...had Dr. Fitzgerald told Aunt Joy about that *other* thing?

It didn't matter that Aunt Joy had probably been drunk as usual, drowning her sorrows away, as she'd been doing ever since Mom and Dad died in a car accident when Grace was twelve. It didn't matter that Aunt Joy had been a stumbling, alcoholic mess since. In the end, Aunt Joy was right. Lilly had died, and Grace had gone running, and then slept it off. She hadn't even bothered to call the funeral home.

Grace sat up, pressing her phone to her ear. "God. Aunt Joy. I'm so sorry. You're right. I should've called, I..." Grace realized she was babbling, so she took a deep breath, gathering herself before she continued. "God, I was so messed up. I wasn't thinking. Dr. Fitzgerald called me right before I was about to run, and..."

Aunt Joy snorted. "*Running. Of course. I should've known. What else could be more important than informing your aunt that her niece has died?*"

Anger flickered inside, warring against her own self-loathing and guilt, but Grace swallowed it down, fighting to keep control. "Aunt Joy. Please. Let's not do this. You're right. I should've called you. I just wasn't thinking..."

"*Of course not. You just wanted to run. Like you always do. Run away from reality. You've been running ever since your parents died, running from the truth of how the real world works. I was slaving away at that awful nursing home when I should've been retired, to support you and Lilly, and all you could do was run away instead of carrying your weight around the house, like a responsible person would've.*"

"Aunt Joy. No. *Please* stop."

"*How could you have not known? Seen what was going to happen? Oh, that's right. You were running away, as usual, while Lilly lowered herself, waiting tables at The Skylark with gutter trash like Cassie Tillman. Well, you just keep running away. I'll handle Lilly's funeral, like the adult you refuse to be.*"

Her anger blossomed and flared to full-fledged life, finally snapping her restraint. "You're the adult? You? God. You're fucking *kidding* me!"

"*You watch your tone...!*"

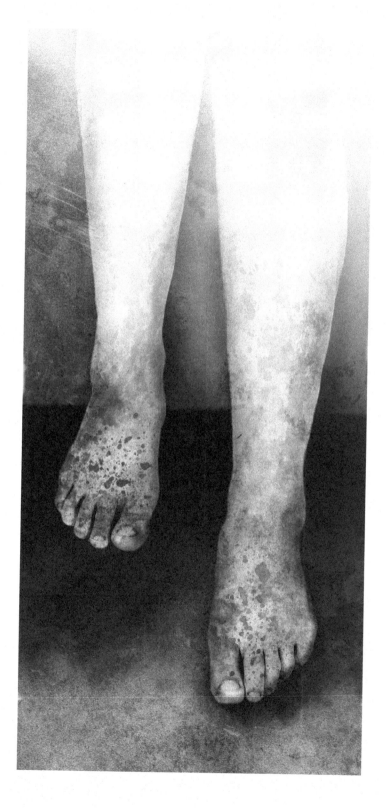

"No," Grace said through gritted teeth, clutching the phone against her ear so hard it hurt. "No. *I'm* the one who found Lilly. *I've* been sitting in the hospital every day, watching her die. *Me.* I've been talking with Dr. Fitzgerald, listening to all his explanations about their useless attempts to save Lilly and how, if she did make it, she'd be a drooling, incontinent vegetable for the rest of her life. *I* had to listen to that. All you've done is occasionally drunk-dial me, sobbing like a *child.* While I handled everything, Aunt Joy. *Me.* Y'know, the funny thing is, Dr. Fitzgerald probably tried to call you right after me, but I bet you were too drunk to answer the phone. That's why you didn't come pounding on my door last night, isn't it? You were probably too blitzed to drive, or to dial my number."

The edges of Lilly's pendant cut into Grace's palm as she squeezed. She hadn't even been aware of grabbing it, but now she clutched it, as if drawing strength from it. As it grew warmer against her skin, that warmth seemed to flow into her, fanning the flames of her burning guilt and rage even higher.

"How dare you...!"

Something cried out inside Grace, a burst of sentiment and her own shame, briefly dousing the roaring fire inside. She was lashing out, she knew. Really, it *had* been negligent of her not to call Aunt Joy. Negligent and selfish. Aunt Joy was their closest relative. Grace should've called her, if only because of the good times they'd shared before her parents' death.

But those good days were gone and buried in her parents' graves, washed away by Aunt Joy's alcoholic descent. Yes, it was negligent of her not to have called Aunt Joy about Lilly, but Aunt Joy had shown plenty of negligence in her time, which was why she and Lilly had moved out of her home to begin with.

Whatever regret Grace felt for her harsh words vanished. "You don't think I handle things? Fine. There's a funeral to plan. Have at it."

Aunt Joy sputtered, unable to form a coherent response. Grace didn't give her a chance, clicking 'End' on her smartphone and tossing it onto her bed. She sat on the edge and covered her face with one hand, her other clutching Lilly's pendant, shaking with a mixture of grief and rage.

Grace breathed deeply and wiped her face. Raked her fingers through her hair and stood up. She'd go run. Harder than she ever had. She'd run it all out of her; the pain, rage and guilt...

Her thoughts trailed off as she looked at her feet. They were stained with dried patches of mud. Pine needles were stuck in the dried mud. Staring at her mysteriously dirtied feet, her mind skipping, she wiggled her toes and felt a tiny prick between her pinkie toe and its neighbor. A small twig was stuck there.

She bent over. Slowly extracted the twig, straightened and stared at it for several seconds.

midwives

Grace breathed in, then out. She shoved aside fleeting memories of last night's dreams. Flicked the twig away and went to get her running shoes on.

6:00 AM

GRACE fought to empty her mind as she turned onto Hyland Avenue. She didn't want to think about Lilly, Aunt Joy's failings or Lilly's funeral, but despite her threats she knew she *couldn't* leave the funeral arrangements to Aunt Joy. Grace would have to handle it, like she'd handled everything else the past six years. Grace owed it to Lilly to handle this last thing, before finally washing her hands of Aunt Joy for good. Until *she* died, of course, and the way she'd been drinking lately…

Empty.

She had to empty her mind. Replace her thoughts with the sound of her breathing, heartbeat and footfalls, the sounds of her body falling into rhythm. She needed to forget, for a moment, Lilly and the funeral arrangements, and *run*.

Houses blurred by, as did cars parked along the curb. She turned left onto Main Street, flying past shops and town buildings. The police station. Town hall. Brooks Pharmacy. Great American Grocery. At the town limits she kept going on Shelby Road, gliding like a well-oiled machine, thinking about *nothing*.

Not Lilly.

Or death or suicide. Or her dream of the night road, or The Thing Which Should Not Be Named, or HIM, above all. She thought about nothing. Not the schoolwork she wasn't doing, or quitting cross country, or about the inevitable hospital and funeral expenses she'd have to somehow pay without insurance. She thought of nothing and existed only in the running.

Ahead she saw the entrance to Shelby Road Cemetery. When she reached it she turned left, down the road through the cemetery, along which she'd stumbled yesterday. This time, however, she adjusted to the terrain smoothly.

She reached the tree line.

Thinking nothing as she plunged through.

THE *Night* ROAD

Early morning light filtered through Adirondack pine. Crisp autumn air nipped pleasantly at her face, stinging her lungs as she breathed. The road inclined, as it had before. Pumping her arms, she crested it easily, stride lengthening to accommodate the rise. As she started down the rise, she likewise shortened her stride, adjusting for the descent.

Down the access road, turning a corner, Grace saw her, vanishing out of sight. Her black hair flashing: the runner in black.

the patient looks at Grace
lets go of the midwife's hand
and takes the runner's

Scattered images of last night's dream flashed in her mind as she ran harder. She remembered the sensation of her feet flying over the ground, the near ecstatic feeling of euphoria singing in her heart as she'd run. Though lacking the surreal, hazy nature of the dream, she felt near that euphoria now as she pursued the runner in black toward the abandoned village at the end of the road. And, though she again figured it was a combination of her imagination and her flushed skin, it felt as if Lilly's pendant throbbed with warmth.

Up ahead Grace saw the rise leading to the abandoned village, and the runner in black disappearing over its top. She was gaining. This realization spurred her into running even harder. Though it didn't seem possible, she sped up with little effort, her heart rate and breathing steady.

In what seemed like no time at all, Grace was clearing the small rise and entering the abandoned village. As Grace crossed the threshold, she experienced a strange vision of ghostly villagers going about their business. It was as if someone had laid a filmstrip of wispy figures over one of the road. The image went as quickly as it came, the images fading into nothingness.

She also expected, at any moment, to hear a chorus of croaks and caws from the branches above her. There was only silence, but she kept running, and didn't look up.

The buildings and cabins flashed by. In her peripheral vision, shadows darted. Though she kept her gaze ahead, she couldn't help imagining the shadows leaning on porch railings or sitting in chairs, washing clothes in tubs or tending gardens, standing in doorways, smoking or drinking.

Grace's thoughts ground to a halt. She abruptly slowed to a jog, then a few steps later, stopped and stared.

The two roads merged into one past the cabins and buildings, continuing on several feet into the woods until it curved left and down a hill, out of sight. That didn't concern her, however. Standing where the roads merged, with her back to Grace, was the mysterious runner in black.

Grace opened her mouth, but nothing came out. As if on cue, the runner turned and smiled. "I was right. Someone was following me."

The woman—who appeared to be only a bit older than Grace—possessed an almost regal face. She had a firm jawline, high cheekbones and an aquiline nose. Her eyes glowed a startling hazel. If she hadn't been smiling, Grace would've felt intimidated, but the woman's friendly tone put her at ease.

"Yeah. Saw you back there," she thumbed behind her, "at the big hill. Seen you a few times the last few days, actually..."

the patient looks at Grace
lets go of the midwife's hand
and takes the runner's

"...just haven't ever caught up with you." Grace swallowed before adding. "You're fast."

The woman tipped her head, her smile widening. "Thanks. I run this path every day. Know the lay of the land, which helps."

Grace nodded. "You were on your way out here, I guess. Do you live in Clifton Heights? I've never seen you around. I mean, I don't know *everyone* in town, but still. It's not that big."

The young woman shook her head. "I'm not from town. Live nearby, though." She paused, her smile turning into a grin. "My name's Morgan."

"Grace. So you run this road a lot?"

Morgan nodded. "Yes. Mostly to see this."

She stepped aside. Grace stared, amazed she hadn't seen this the last time she'd been here. Of course, she hadn't made it all the way through the village before that weird thing with all those crows…but still.

Behind Morgan lay what looked like a modestly-sized graveyard, but instead of gravestones, Grace saw odd, conical piles of rocks meticulously stacked to the relative height of tombstones. Sitting in line with each other, the piles looks as if they'd been laid out on a grid. Grace guessed forty at least, but if she took the time to make a more careful count, she figured she'd find more.

As she stared, an amazing sense of peace settled over her. Lilly's death and Aunt Joy's drinking faded even further in the face of the rock piles. They looked ancient. Timeless, even.

"It's amazing, isn't it? Peaceful. Transcendent, almost."

Grace blinked, startled to hear Morgan talking so close to her. She'd been staring so intently at the rock piles that she hadn't noticed the woman coming near.

"Those rock piles. What are they?"

"Cairns."

A chill rippled down Grace's spine, the word sounding as ancient as the rock piles looked. "Cairns?"

THE *Night* ROAD

"Traditional Irish grave-markers."

Grace frowned slightly, confused. "If they're Irish, what are they doing *here?*" She turned and faced the abandoned village behind her. "What *is* this place? Do you know anything about it?"

"I do. May seem strange, but there are cairns in many places like these, throughout the Adirondacks. In the '30s and '40s Irish immigrants settled in Adirondack Park and worked as laborers. Mining, logging, construction. You name it. They worked wherever they could, but they wanted to keep to themselves and their way of life. Observe their own beliefs and burial customs. Hence the cairns, and what remains of this small village here. You could do that back then, without town bureaucracy getting in the way."

Morgan turned and faced the village remains. "*This* small hamlet in particular was unique. Did you know the road opens into the far side of Raedeker Park Zoo?"

Raedeker Park Zoo was off Samara Hill Road, which was a left about a mile or so before Shelby Road Cemetery, so Grace figured that made sense. "No, I didn't. Why?"

"In the thirties and forties, Raedeker Park Zoo was Raedeker Park Zoo & *Carnival*. The Irish who lived in this little village worked in the zoo and at the carnival as carnies. The carnival closed in the seventies. An accident on several of the rides caused controversy and cost the park too much money, so Raedeker Park shut down the carnival, then tore down the rides. It wasn't long before most of the young folks from this hamlet left. The rest, those too old to travel or look for work elsewhere…" Morgan shrugged, looking over the old buildings with an odd expression of regret, "they stayed until they eventually passed on. They're most likely buried here, with the rest of their townsfolk who'd gone before them."

"How do you know all this?"

Morgan gave her a wry smile. "Folklore is my specialty."

Grace nodded, staring at the cairns, suddenly conflicted, her peace disturbed. *Burial* of course led to thoughts of graveyards and funerals which, despite her best efforts, led her thoughts back to Lilly, Aunt Joy, and funeral arrangements which still needed to be made.

Lilly was dead.

It was her fault.

Time to stop playing explorer and get about the business she should be attending to: arranging Lilly's final resting place.

"Look," Grace said with forced cheer, trying to disperse her suddenly serious thoughts, "It's been nice meeting you…but I should get going. Are you…" she nodded back to the cemetery.

Morgan shook her head. "I'm going to take some time. Be alone with the cairns."

"Oh. Okay. Well. Maybe I'll run here again tomorrow. Will I see you?"

Morgan's smile brightened. "I'd like that."

Suddenly out of words, terribly aware of time passing, Grace waved. "Okay. Maybe tomorrow, then."

Morgan nodded, still smiling. "Tomorrow."

Grace nodded. She turned awkwardly and walked away, reluctance dogging her every step down the access road and past the old buildings. She didn't want to leave Morgan. Didn't want to go back to town.

But she had to.

She ran away, drawn by duty, obligation and guilt.

———

WHEN she returned home, instead of showering and changing, Grace got into her car, intending to head straight to the funeral home. She had to beat Aunt Joy there, or at the very least, get there in time to prevent Aunt Joy from ruining Lilly's funeral.

In some part of her mind, Grace questioned just exactly *how* Aunt Joy could possibly ruin Lilly's funeral. Pay for the wrong kind of coffin? Go cheap and purchase a plot plaque instead of a headstone? Did any of that really matter? All Aunt Joy had to do was make a few requests, fork over some money, and the funeral home would take care of the rest.

No, deep inside, as she sat in her idling car, Grace knew she wanted to get there before Aunt Joy for purely selfish reasons. She wanted to handle the funeral, to show Aunt Joy she *could*. She was Lilly's closest living relative. *She* should handle Lilly's final affairs.

Well, she whispered to herself in a voice which sounded remarkably like Aunt Joy's, *if you wanted to do that so bad, you should've gone straight to the funeral home instead of going out for a run.*

Grace looked into the rear-view mirror, realizing for the first time how much she looked like a younger version of Aunt Joy. For a split second, she wondered what life would be like floating numbly through a warm liquor haze, and she hated the appeal of that thought.

Grace was about to look away in disgust when a pinprick flare in the mirror caught her eye. She looked closer and realized the sun was reflecting off Lilly's pendant. The pendant Lilly had bought two months ago at Handy's Pawn and Thrift, which she'd worn every day and night since, and which Grace had felt compelled to start wearing two days ago.

She touched the pendant. Rubbed it between her thumb and forefinger. Thought very hard. And, despite every ounce of common sense demanding she race to the funeral home, Grace put her car into gear and headed to Handy's Pawn and Thrift.

THE *Night* ROAD

—

SHE couldn't get out of her car immediately, however, as it idled at the curb outside Handy's. Now that she was here, she felt incredibly foolish. Stupid, even. For all she knew, Aunt Joy was at the funeral home right now, or maybe she was already finished, the arrangements made.

It was a stupid waste of time. She needed to get to Quiet Meadows Funeral Home. Her hand was on the shift, about to put her car into gear, when she looked up once more and found her gaze caught by the gold letters on the store's maroon sign:

Handy's Pawn and Thrift
We Have
Things You Need

Damn.

She couldn't get past it, though all her common sense told her to. What had possessed Lilly to buy a necklace *here*, of all places? Why had she felt compelled to wear it all the time, and why had *she* started wearing it? What did the etchings mean? Did she imagine the pendant's strange warmth, or…?

It's just a necklace.

That's all.

Grace stared at the sign for a heartbeat longer.

Things You Need

"Screw it," she muttered. She shut the car off and got out.

—

"GOOD morning. How can I help you? Looking for anything in particular?"

Grace stood still for a moment, not answering, examining the inside of Handy's. She'd only ever been inside once or twice as a kid, and she must not have seen anything very memorable, because she didn't recognize the store at all. Indeed, she saw nothing very remarkable now, only rows of shelves cluttered with the things people dumped on tables at lawn sales. Old tools, toys, cameras, mugs, glasses and plates. Far as she could tell, there seemed to be no discernible order to the store's arrangement, with the exception of the clothing racks in the far left corner.

On the sales counter sat a glass display case which, from her vantage point, looked filled with odds and ends of jewelry. Had Lilly chosen her necklace and its pendant from there?

"Excuse me, miss?"

With great effort Grace focused on the voice. Squinting, she saw a tall form smoothly move from

arranging clothes on the racks to stand in the aisle running down the middle of the store.

Grace swallowed and approached the man, feeling slightly awed and even a little uneasy, though she had no idea why. He looked friendly enough. Charming, even. Tall and robust with wide shoulders, but not overweight. The man—who must be the store's owner—looked like an ex-quarterback who'd never quite lost his battle with old age. His white hair and beard were neatly trimmed, but his face was devoid of wrinkles, save faint crow's feet at the corners of his startling blue eyes. He seemed like a kindly yet vibrant uncle, but also something *more*. What, she had no idea, and she couldn't put her finger on the unease he inspired in her.

Still, she'd come this far and wasted this much time, might as well go all the way. Aunt Joy had more than likely finished Lilly's affairs. Might as well commit, though she still had no idea why finding out more about Lilly's pendant seemed so important.

"Yes. Sorry. Spaced out there for a minute. Are you the store owner? I was wondering if you could tell me more about an item my sister bought here a few months ago. A necklace."

The man tipped his head graciously. "I'll do my best. I remember most of the items which travel through here, but occasionally my memory betrays me. It's to be expected at my age."

He held up a finger. "As to your first question, however. No, I'm not the owner. Merely one of Mr. Handy's many and humble shopkeepers."

Something in the man's smile and manner washed away her strange unease. Grace wondered why she'd ever felt it to begin with. As she approached the counter, she tugged on the necklace, pulling it and its pendant out from under her shirt. Without taking it off (because strangely the thought of removing it made her feel panicky) she held up the pendant and said, "My sister Lilly bought this a few months ago. She fell in love with it and wore it all the time, though she never said why. Was wondering if you knew anything about it."

"Ah. Yes, I remember it well." The shopkeeper stepped closer and took the pendant from Grace, holding it between his thumb and forefinger. He rubbed it, peering closely. "I sold this to Lilly Donaldson." A light of recognition blossomed in his eyes. "And that makes you Grace Donaldson."

She nodded, knowing what came next, and hating every bit of it.

"Best runner to come out of Clifton Heights. Besides your father, Will Donaldson. All-County since freshman year; Webb County Runner of the Year two years in a row. And, I believe Section Three Cross-Country State Champion, one of those years."

THE *Night* ROAD

Grace nodded tightly, trying to keep her face neutral, choking back the bile she always tasted when a random stranger praised her running accolades. Thankfully, the shopkeeper seemed content to stop there and continue his examination of Lilly's pendant. "Yes, Lilly came in about two months ago, as you said. I believe she was merely killing time to begin with. So many people come here for only that, at first. She was eventually drawn to the jewelry case on the counter, and then this item in particular. Soon as she picked it up, I knew she'd be buying it. She was taken by it. Even said she'd felt *called* by it."

Grace thought of her odd notion to start wearing it herself, and how at times it seemed to pulse with warmth, even give her strength. "Does it…mean anything? Is it…" she paused, feeling foolish, "special?"

"Yes, very much so. It's hard to see at first, but if you look very closely…" He held up the pendant so Grace could see, "…at these etchings, you'll see they form mirror images of what look like birds. More specifically…"

"Crows," she rasped, finally seeing what the etchings on the small silver disc formed.

"Why yes," the shopkeeper remarked with some surprise. "Ravens, actually. As I told your sister, if memories of my university days serve me right, this is the ancient signifier for the Morrigan, or Morrigu, from Irish mythology."

Irish immigrants

settled in Adirondack Park

Somehow Grace kept her voice level. "What's the Morrigan?"

The shopkeeper regarded the pendant even more closely. "The Phantom Queen, I believe. Goddess of Fate and Death. Stories call her The Watcher of the Cairns, the Guardian of the Night Road. Cairns are..."

Grace nodded slowly, like she was stuck in a fever dream. "Traditional Irish grave-markers."

The shopkeeper raised his eyebrows. "Right again. Someone's been studying their Irish mythology. The Morrigan—the Phantom Queen—guarded the cairns and the roads leading to them, which were often called ley lines, faerie paths, or night roads. They were routes of elemental magic connecting sites of power: Churches, places of pagan worship, sites of great death or historical importance, and graveyards."

Shelby Road Cemetery

"Among other things, the Morrigan supposedly ferried lost souls—both alive and dead—to the afterlife along the night road."

"*Alive* and dead?"

"Yes. Sometimes those who had lost their way in life, lost their purpose, would travel the night road, and the Morrigan would gather them up, to run with them forever. At least, so the stories say."

THE *Night* ROAD

Grace breathed deep and pulled herself back from some chasm inside, an abyss filled with fantastic images of running at night, inexplicably dirty feet in the morning, and a twig stuck between her toes. "Run forever? Doesn't sound so awful." She shivered; what she'd meant as a flip comment had come out far more serious than she'd intended. "Too bad they're only stories."

The shopkeeper smiled, released the pendant back into Grace's hand, and clasped his before him. "Indeed. On an interesting side-note: old abandoned villages often lay on night roads. In the old country they were called *TírnanÓg*. Means 'Land of Youth' or 'Otherworld.' They were known as portals to night roads. Gateways, of sorts." He tipped his head, and now his smile seemed strange, and again Grace felt uneasy in his presence. "Woe to mortals who violated the sanctity of these places, however. The Morrigan did not deal with them lightly."

Grace looked at the pendant—the mirror ravens now unmistakable—before placing it back under her shirt. "Thank you." She turned away and walked slowly down the aisle to the door.

As she grasped the doorknob, the shopkeeper called out, "It's highly ironic, as I told your sister. Almost kismet, in a way. Which makes even more sense, given she's the Goddess of Fate, the Morrigan."

Grace paused but resisted the urge to look over her shoulder. Her misgivings about the shopkeeper had returned in full, and she didn't want to look at him. "What is?"

"That Lilly would be drawn to such an item, and seeing as how you're now wearing it, that you would be drawn to it also. My condolences, by the way."

Grace's mind stuttered, the shopkeeper's odd knowledge of Lilly's passing barely registering. "Why is it ironic?"

"Well, I wouldn't know for sure of course, and perhaps you don't even know...but your last name. Donaldson. It's a common Anglicization of the *Irish* name McDonnells."

Grace nodded slowly, for some reason not surprised at this information. "Thank you again," she whispered, pulling the door open and leaving the store.

———

AFTER her encounter with Morgan...

The Phantom Queen

...and her impromptu visit to Handy's Pawn and Thrift, it was going on eleven in the morning. Surely Aunt Joy had beaten her to the funeral home, had come and gone already, but Grace couldn't make herself drive any faster. Too many ideas and images swirled and clashed in her

head. The necklace and its pendant, apparently an old...
what had the shopkeeper called it?...signifier for some sort
of Irish goddess. The Morrigan. Morrigu. The Phantom
Queen. The runner in black, whose name was Morgan,
who had taken Lilly's hand as she died in a dream, and the
cairn. The abandoned village, the access road...

Ley lines.

Night roads.

Otherworlds. She couldn't push the thoughts away,
couldn't organize them as they tumbled and spun in her
mind, hitting each other, bouncing off and...

The abandoned town.

Ghost images from the corner of her eye.

The crows. All the crows.

TírnanÓg.

Morgan, the runner in black, who she'd seen right
after putting on Lilly's necklace for the first time.
Donaldson? Did it used to be something else? Was she
Irish? What did it all *mean*? What was happening to...

Grace's heart clenched as she pulled up to Quiet
Meadows Funeral Home. In the parking lot stood Aunt
Joy. Arms crossed over chest, holding herself rigidly,
glaring at Grace as she pulled into the parking lot and
parked her Escort.

Shame burned inside Grace. She should've gotten here
first thing in the morning, before Aunt Joy could arrive.

She should've been *here*, handling things. Instead she'd
spent the morning running, talking with a stranger...

Morgan

The Phantom Queen

...and chasing fairy tales at a junk shop.

Grace sat in her idling Escort, hands tightening
on the wheel as she tried to pull herself together. The
sooner she finished this, the sooner she could run to that
abandoned village...

run the night road

...and find Morgan.

She wasn't surprised at her intentions. She wanted
to return to the cairns and the abandoned village in the
woods as soon as she could. *Needed* to return. She had
questions about things she could barely articulate. The
necklace. The Morrigan. Crows, ley lines, family names
and the night road. Silly to think Morgan could answer
those questions...

The Phantom Queen

folklore is my specialty

...but she needed to return all the same, because
it was *more* than Morgan. It was the *stillness* she'd felt
around the cairn and in the village. The way she'd felt
running on the access road leading there, the sense of
purpose and freedom and...

the night road

THE *Night* ROAD

Her run home had felt awkward and unnatural, and she hadn't enjoyed it at all. Her muscles had cooled down and her joints had stiffened up. Something else had been missing, too. A rhythm. A feeling. The harmonious bliss she'd felt while running the access road. She wanted that back, as soon as possible. She wanted peace, she wanted to be near Morgan, she wanted to...

Run forever.

Grace clenched her jaw. Morgan and questions would have to wait. The reality of arranging Lilly's funeral and grappling with Aunt Joy over the details had to be dealt with *now*. Taking a deep breath, Grace shut off the car and got out.

9

BEFORE Grace could open her mouth, Aunt Joy snapped at her. "Where have you *been*? First, you don't call me to say my niece—your *sister*—is dead. Second, you blow off this morning and disappear when you should be helping me with the funeral arrangements."

Aunt Joy's eyes narrowed. "Were you running while I handled everything?"

Sadness swelled in Grace's heart. How had things fallen this far? When Mom and Dad had been alive, Aunt Joy had been fun and carefree. She'd taken her and Lilly to the movies and the summer carnival, had them over for sleepovers in the backyard. But Dad's death had damaged something deep inside Aunt Joy, and she'd never recovered. It had killed the woman they'd known, replacing her with an increasingly harsh, bitter, alcoholic drudge who had treated them more and more like boarders, not family.

Aunt Joy scowled, eyebrows arching. "Well? Were you running while I was here being the grown-up and handling your sister's funeral arrangements?"

Grace only barely suppressed a flash of anger inside. So her parents' death had hurt Aunt Joy. So what? How much more had it hurt *them*?

Even so, Aunt Joy was family. The only family Grace had left. Swallowing, she said tightly, "Aunt Joy. I'm sorry. You're right. I should've been here. I don't have any excuse. I was just..."

Aunt Joy glared at her. "You were just *running*. That's all you ever do. All you've ever cared about. It's no wonder Lilly's dead. You were too busy running to notice your own sister was planning to..."

Her face reddened as she trailed off, unable to finish the accusation. Grace tensed and felt, very distantly, Lilly's pendant...

the signifier of the Morrigan

...throbbing warmly, searing her skin. It came in a flash, a thought so vile and poisonous her stomach twisted in pain.

THE *Night* ROAD

I hate you

And on the heels of that traitorous thought, she saw herself, so very clearly, cocking her injured right hand and delivering a roundhouse punch—fueled by all her pain and anger and guilt and grief—which jerked Aunt Joy's head to the left and almost knocked her down. In that flash she felt her reopened wounds sting and bleed, and saw faint streaks of red on Aunt Joy's cheek.

She blinked.

A storm of angry confusion raging in her head.

Aunt Joy's face was clear. No blood on her cheeks. Grace's fist was clenched at her side, having only been swung in her mind. Aunt Joy's eyes had widened, however, much of her bluster vanished, as if she'd sensed the blackness surging in Grace's heart and had seen the violence in her eyes.

Unsure of her ability to control the emotions boiling inside, Grace backed away toward her car. Aunt Joy took a tentative step after, her fighting spirit seemingly drained by the malice she must've felt rolling off Grace.

Grace backed up another step.

Aunt Joy blinked and rasped,

"Grace. Oh, Grace, I'm so…I didn't mean…"

Grace shut out Aunt Joy's pleas and spun away. She grasped her Escort's door handle, flung the door open and threw herself inside, slamming the door behind her.

She grappled with her keys, stuck them into the ignition and turned them, ignoring the muffled sobs outside.

The engine caught. She slammed it into gear and backed out of the funeral home's turnaround, pulled out onto the street and raced away, to the only place left on earth she wanted to be. So intent was she on her goal she didn't stop at the intersection past the funeral home but sped through, barely registering a squeal of tires and a loud, growling engine.

——

GRACE parked near Shelby Road Cemetery's gates. For a moment, she considered turning into the cemetery and driving down the access road, but she instantly rejected the notion. She didn't know why, but the thought of *driving* down the access road disgusted her. The road to the cairns was meant for running. Not *driving*.

She switched the ignition off, grabbed the steering wheel with both hands and twisted as hard as she could. She sobbed harshly as a black storm raged inside her. She squeezed her eyes shut, trying to shut out the images of what she'd almost done, what she'd *wanted* to do.

She saw again, with picture-perfect clarity, her fist smashing into Aunt Joy's face. Saw Aunt Joy's head jerk with the blow. Experienced again a malignant flash of *satisfaction* as her knuckles connected with her aunt's chin, nearly drowning in the guilt and shame welling up inside over what she'd wanted to do to her only surviving relative…who'd been *right*, all along.

all you could do was run away

That was all she'd ever done, since *IT* happened. Run away. Pretended she hadn't seen anything, and run away, as far as she could, from the truth.

Dear God, Aunt Joy was right.

She was right.

sometimes those who had lost their way

they would travel the night road

the Morrigan would gather them up, to run with them forever

Grace swallowed her guilt and self-loathing as she pushed the driver's side door open. She exited and headed for the cemetery gates, leaving her keys in the ignition and the driver side door open. She knew she'd never drive her car again. It was an instinct she didn't question.

Had she *really* wanted to strike Aunt Joy…or had it been *him* she wanted to hurt? Had she been mentally lashing out at Aunt Joy as a replacement for a target she couldn't hit? At this point, she realized it didn't matter. The overwhelming peace she felt earlier at the cairn and the abandoned village was returning. Soon she'd be there with Morgan, and she wouldn't care about anything else. What that meant she wasn't exactly sure…

run forever

…but she didn't care about anything else, now.

She was passing through the cemetery gates when she heard it thrumming down the road toward her. The throaty rumble of a pick-up truck, one she knew far too well.

No.

She recognized it from the intersection she'd just sped through.

Him.

She remembered the truck she thought had been following her home from the hospital.

He's been following me!

She turned and saw the restored red '74 Chevy pull up and stop with a jerk. The engine cut off and he clambered out. His expression set Grace on edge. She saw desperation mixed with frustration on his features, his eyes wild and glittering. Even more alarming: he'd parked between her and her car. As she edged down the access road toward the woods, she noted he, like her, was dressed to run. Of course, he was always dressed to run.

He stepped forward, seemingly caught between sympathy and irritation. "Grace. Listen to me. I need to know. Just tell me what I need to know, and then I'm gone. Out of your life for good, I promise."

She backed up another step, quiet terror rippling down her spine, speeding her heart and breath. Adrenaline

spiked through her, but she wasn't sure if she could run. Her legs felt like rubber. She was afraid they'd collapse beneath her.

"No," she rasped. "You've got no right to ask me that."

"Please." He took another step toward her. "I need to know if she said anything about…us. Did she…did she kill herself because…because of…"

"NO!" Grace screamed at him, her muscles tensing, no longer trembling with fear. "You've got no right!"

"I have to know! I…"

Grace turned and sprinted away, down the road toward the woods. Her heart hammered and her breath roared. All her fear, anger and guilt flowed through her, propelling her forward, even as she heard his thudding footfalls in pursuit.

———

Trees flashed by. Sunlight flickered through their branches. Her feet flew over the ground, every part of her working together in a way she'd never known. Fear drove her forward, but not *just* fear, a part of her singing with the running. Running was everything, and she wanted to do it forever.

But she could hear him gaining.

He was faster than her. Always had been. He was catching up to her, as they both sped up the rise.

At the top, she heard a grunt, then felt his hands on her arms and a shoulder in her back. He'd lunged the last few steps up the rise and grabbed her. The impact threw her forward. Her feet tangled with his. They both fell, their mingled shouts echoing as they rolled down the path to the hill's bottom. His hands never let go. They were clamped onto her biceps. A mind-numbing terror filled her as they fell. They'd land with her on the bottom, him on top, and then he'd...

They tumbled to a stop at the bottom of the hill.

Her head struck a rock.

Sharp pain squeezed her head in a terrible vise.

Blackness rushed in, and she felt as if she were running forever in the dark...

———

GRACE feels as if she's flying, her feet gliding over the night road as she runs forever, running away from the world and all her pain, away from death and failure and guilt and shame...

She runs with power and strength and might, and she wants to run like this, always. Run, and never think again, exist only in the running, nothing else...

Something roars above her.

THE *Night* ROAD

A deep-throated screech which makes the air vibrate and the trees shudder. A great flapping, a rush of air which almost knocks Grace over, and It lands in her way, barring the night road.

She slides to a stop, gasping at the sight before her. The impossible creature sits taller than her, covered with black down and feathers, but the word feathers seems common, falling short of the truth. It spreads wings which must equal the span of a small plane and regards her with molten, golden, intelligent eyes.

It falls silent, sitting in the night road, massive wings blocking the way. It stares at her with a smoldering intensity.

Curiously Grace feels no fear. She approaches It slowly and surely. As she draws near, It opens Its beak and utters a rasping croak which rumbles in Its breast and sounds less like a warning, and more like…a query.

Or an invitation.

Grace stands before It. In an oddly subservient motion, It lowers Its head, placing Its golden yellow beak level with her head. She reaches out an amazingly firm and steady hand. Places it flat on the cool smoothness of Its beak, never once fearing It might strike, or take her hand. When she speaks, it's without a tremor, the words springing from an unknown place deep inside her, sounding strange yet familiar in her mouth at the same time.

"Let me pass," she whispers, full of a longing she can't understand. "Let me run on the night road, where I belong. Where I need to be. Let me run here forever."

She withdraws her hand.

It raises Its head, lifts Its beak to the sky and doesn't caw but roars in triumph—or acceptance, she doesn't know—as something screams into her ears, *Tell me...*

———

HANDS shook her roughly. Pain throbbed in her head, spiking with each word he yelled.

"Tell me! You have to know! You *have* to! Tell me!"

Insane fear woke her all the way up and dampened the pain, propelling Grace to her feet. She lunged away from him but he still held tight and jerked her back.

"Tell me!" No longer trying to act concerned or sympathetic, frightened rage twisted his face into a cruel snarl. "I have a right to know!"

"Fuck you!" Grace pushed him, hands flat against his chest, hard enough to knock him back several feet, but his fingers were still clutching her biceps. He dragged her with him. "You don't deserve to know!"

The anger in his face faded, some part of him still sane, maybe. "Listen, I know you don't understand. But what she and I had...it was...special...it..."

"She *trusted* you! *I* trusted you! It wasn't special…it was wrong! It was sick!"

He shook her, snarling. "Don't say that! You don't know! You don't!"

Grace flailed, trying to punch him, scratch his eyes out, gouge his cheeks, anything to make him let her go. "You were her *coach!* You were my coach! You taught me how to run, how to win! YOU RUINED EVERYTHING! I HATE YOU!"

He shook her again, sneering, pressing his face close to hers. "Why didn't you say something, then? You knew. I *know* you did! Why didn't you say anything, if you thought it was so wrong?"

Shame and guilt burned like twin suns inside of her. Grace opened her mouth but she couldn't speak. Tears held back for too long finally flooded her eyes. "I didn't want you to stop teaching me. I…" she whimpered and looked away. "I couldn't…you taught me everything about running, I wanted you to keep…keep teaching me…didn't want…didn't want to lose…"

Her fault.

Lilly was dead.

It was her fault.

She'd said nothing.

And Lilly was dead.

"Did she do it because of me? Because of us? Did she do it…because of the *baby?*"

127

Time stopped.

As if the world had taken in a breath, and was now holding it. The thing—the other thing, which Dr. Fitzgerald had so gently probed about, which she'd repeatedly refused to discuss—was out, now. In front of her, where she couldn't deny it any longer.

Lilly's baby. Her two-month-old fetus. Now dead, inside of her.

She gasped.

Swallowed and shook her head. She tried to raise her hands to wipe the tears from her eyes, but was unable to because he kept jerking them down. "I...I don't know. She never said anything about it. I...I didn't even know until..." She forced herself to meet his bright, mad gaze. "Until the doctor...the doctor told me about it after she..."

His jaw tensed and his face hardened, eyes dancing madly. "I don't believe you. You're *lying*."

She knew, then. He was crazy. Whatever he felt—guilt, shame, fear—had driven him insane, because he thought Lilly had tried to kill herself because of him, because he'd gotten her pregnant.

"No. I swear. She never said anything." Grace tugged but he wouldn't let go. "Never."

He jerked her back up the path. She planted her feet, but he was too strong, and he dragged her further. "I need to know what she told you, what she said. Tell me, and everything will be fine."

She saw it in his glittering eyes. Nothing would be fine. Regardless of what she told him, he wasn't planning on letting her leave these woods. She had no idea how he thought he'd get away with it, but maybe it didn't matter. Most likely he was past the point of caring.

Desperate fear threatened to consume her, but Lilly's pendant blazed against her skin, turning her fear into rage. She flung herself *at* him, dropping her shoulder into his chest. It rocked him back on his heels. Without thinking she took advantage and jammed a knee between his legs, hard.

He bent over double, gasping for air. His hold on her relaxed just long enough.

She broke free and fled up the path. She must've caught him with only a glancing blow, either that or his madness was blunting the pain, because he roared and stumbled after her. She could hear him getting closer. If she could clear the rise, maybe find a rock or something...

The small rise loomed ahead, leading to the abandoned village and the cairns. Maybe there were tools in one of the cabins, a shovel or a rake, or...

She ran harder than ever.

He pounded behind her, breath ragged.

She crested the rise...

And the world was filled with black flapping and screeching, feathers flying, claws grasping.

Grace screamed. She slid and fell on her back, arms covering her face. Something large beat the air as it soared over her. Instinctively she thought of It, the thing too majestic to be called a mere bird but that was impossible, it had only been a dream...

Grace rolled over onto her stomach, screaming his name, even after everything he'd done...

It slammed into him as he was clearing the rise. Grace couldn't see Its claws digging into his chest, but she heard his tortured screams. Heard It beat him with Its larger-than-possible wings, heard Its beak snapping...

A bright red geyser spurt from his neck.

He gurgled, hands flailing.

It screeched again, lifted him off the ground and carried him down the rise, out of sight.

She could still hear. Liquid ripping and tearing of flesh. His final weak, gurgling mewls.

And then a contented, leisurely munching, which seemed to last forever.

Grace lay on the ground, shivering, her mind frozen in terror and unbelief. Part of her wanted to scream at the horrible tearing sounds...

Another part of her felt *safe*.

Protected. For the first time in forever.

She heard a flutter of something like wings flapping and folding. Then footsteps, slow and measured, up the rise.

Grace saw the black hair first. Loose and free, not in a ponytail anymore but flowing around an aristocratic face with high cheekbones and an aquiline nose. Glowing, golden eyes gazed at her and a firm, determined mouth, smeared with blood, smiled.

Morgan walked toward her. As she moved, Grace noticed her black windbreaker and running tights rippling with the roll and flex of her muscles. Not like garments at all, more like a second skin, or a layer of black down...and she wasn't wearing running shoes; her yellow feet appeared hard and pebbly, and there were only three toes, not five, and they were much too long and sharp for toes, they were more like...

Morgan stood before her and smiled. Demurely, she wiped her mouth with the back of her hand. She licked her lips and regarded the blood thoughtfully as she spoke.

"I warned you away twice. You returned both times. You then asked for passage on the night road. I will ask again, one last time. *Do* you wish passage unto the night road?"

There was no question. "Yes."

Morgan extended her hand, still stained with his blood, the blood she'd wiped from her mouth. "Then run with me. Forever on the night road. Never feel anything ever again, except the running."

Grace looked at Morgan's hand. "Will I find Lilly?"

Morgan's smiled widened. "She's already running, as I think you know. Catch up with her, and run together forever."

Grace thought for only a moment. About Aunt Joy. About Lilly, hanging from the ceiling fan in her room, and of the day she was running in the woods behind the school and almost stumbled upon her track coach—her instructor, her mentor, her friend, her *surrogate* father— thrusting and grunting like an animal over a quiet and passive Lilly, while Lilly lay staring at Grace with unseeing eyes.

She thought about how she'd done nothing, or said anything, ever.

let me run on the night road

She took Morgan's hand.

Made in USA - North Chelmsford, MA
1309268_9781587678158
03.23.2022 0951